Avry's Magical Cat:

A Marshmallow the Magic Cat Adventure

Written by Dr. Kimberly Brayman

Illustrated by Irina Denissova

For information regarding permission please write to:

Dr. Kimberly Brayman: info@KimberlyBraymanAuthor.com

For bulk and wholesale orders please email Dr. Kimberly Brayman: info@KimberlyBraymanAuthor.com

ISBN: 978-1-951688-11-0 (paperback)

Written by Dr. Kimberly Brayman

Illustrated by Irina Denissova

First Edition

Team Published with Artistic Warrior

Dedicated to my granddaughter who has not yet arrived from the land of fairies and elves.

Table of Contents

Avry's Magical Cat: A Marshmallow the Magic Cat Adventure

Marshmallow Is His Name

It may have been magic helping Avry the day her mama took her to the animal shelter. Avry felt somehow pulled down the aisles. Then she stopped and smiled. He was the one. She looked into his beautiful green eyes.

"Hello. My name is Marshmallow. I'm pleased to meet you," said a very large, very orange cat.

Avry turned to her mama. "I found him Mama! This is my cat and his name is Marshmallow."

"Avry, only white cats are called Marshmallow." Avry's mama was a little perplexed. "Why don't you choose another name? What about Marmalade? He has such beautiful billowing marmalade-colored fur," she said.

Avry crossed her arms and stuck out her little pointed chin. "Mama, I didn't choose his name. He looked in my eyes and told me his name. Marshmallow is his name."

Her mama knew her daughter well and knew there would be no name change for this big, unquestionably orange cat. She sighed and went to fill out the paperwork.

When Marshmallow was just a kitten, a kind fairy gave him the gift of magic. It's also when he got the name Marshmallow, but that's another story for another day.

Now Marshmallow was all grown up. He knew it was time to meet someone special, his person, someone magical inside. That's when, as if by magic, he was scooped up and taken to the animal shelter.

"When Mama finishes the paperwork, you can come home with us," she said as she stroked the cat's soft fur.

Marshmallow turned his head. With one eye looking up and one eye looking down he replied, "I am yours, and you are mine. It was meant to be."

When all the paperwork was done, they brought a crate out for Marshmallow. Avry refused to let anyone put Marshmallow in a carrying crate. She stooped down and picked up her cat.

Marshmallow smiled to himself. He was going where he belonged. He knew he'd feel loved and secure with Avry. He hoped they lived in a farmhouse.

When they pulled up to his new home, Marshmallow could hardly believe his luck. It was a farmhouse! Avry immediately took Marshmallow up to her room. She watched as he explored the room. Then he sat perfectly still, and listened. His green eyes were open wide and his crooked left ear sat up as straight as possible. Avry watched closely and then listened with him.

After a moment, Avry spoke. "I think I can hear the footsteps of fairies." She pressed her ear down on the old wooden floor in her bedroom. Her eyes grew round. "Marshmallow, I hear squeaks. I think the fairies are whispering."

Marshmallow nodded. He could hear them too. He was so happy he had found a new magical best friend.

The Bunnies Are Dancing

Avry woke early one morning. She slowly stretched her arms up and out of the warm, cozy covers. The night sky had not quite said goodbye, and the sun was still yawning in the lake. She sighed with pleasure. No school for twelve days.

"Isn't it wonderful?" she said to Marshmallow. "Twelve days away from that noisy place."

Marshmallow sat on her window ledge. He peered down the leafy mountainside, ever so carefully licking his paws. "Look, Avry," Marshmallow said.

Avry quickly moved soundlessly beside him. "Oh, Marshmallow, the bunnies are dancing this morning. I wonder if I can dance with them?" she asked wistfully.

Marshmallow blinked and pointed with his left paw. That was something he and Avry had in common—they were both left-handed. Avry looked to where Marshmallow pointed. An old hoot owl with giant wings flew by. "Good morning. Good morning," it hooted.

"Look closer at the owl," Marshmallow said. Avry gasped when she saw what Marshmallow saw. "Is that a little fairy? A little elf? Who is on his back, Marshmallow?"

"I think it's a fairy," said Marshmallow. "I can see its wings."

That was another thing Avry and Marshmallow had in common. They could both see magical things. Avry knew Marshmallow was magical. Her nana had told her, "Avry, if you look past what you think you can see, you will see his magic. In fact, you will see all the magic in the world."

Avry wished everyone knew the things Nana had taught her. "Marshmallow," Avry said, as they watched the owl fly away, "I am the luckiest girl alive to have a magical friend like you."

Marshmallow smiled. Avry's nana knew who he was. Avry did too. It felt good to have someone look inside, and see who he really was.

Too Many People

Sometimes, Avry's family had company over. The voices made her head hurt. Today was one of those days. She sat near the top of the rickety farmhouse steps. "Oh, Marshmallow," she said, "let's stay up here." With her knees drawn up, and her blond hair going this way and that, she caught glimpses of the guests. "Neighbors," she thought. "I'll have to talk to them. Ugh! Let's not go down." Marshmallow nodded and the pair sat quietly and watched.

Avry didn't know how to tell her parents or teachers that she loved people, but any more than three felt like too many. Avry wondered why she needed to be social anyway.

She had Marshmallow, Nana, and her oldest friend, Stefan and his dog, Shadow. They could all see magic, and for Avry, that was enough.

Most people made her tired inside. Her mama told her she was an introvert.

Avry stroked Marshmallow's fur. "Is being an introvert good or bad?" Sometimes new words scared her.

"Avry, that is the perfect way for you," Marshmallow said in as soft a voice as possible. "I know it feels hard sometimes when there are groups of people, but all that means is that you are sensitive and intuitive. You think about a lot of fabulous things."

Marshmallow was right. Avry often knew what people were feeling or thinking, and she did have some fabulous ideas.

Dr. Kimberly Brayman

Being an introvert was hard. School was so loud and so bright that she wanted to hide under her desk. Sometimes when children were listening to the teacher, she just wanted to be dancing with Marshmallow, and twirl in a pretty dress. Knowing he was waiting at home for her made her days better. Thank goodness she still had a few more days before she had to go back to school.

Wishing For A Fairy Teacher

Avry and Marshmallow were so much alike. They did not want to hear the alarm clock—too loud; her mother calling—too insistent; or the toot of the school bus horn—too impatient. They wanted time to sit quietly and watch for the elves who lived in the big tree outside.

"Marshmallow, if a fairy teacher comes to school, I might listen better," Avry said dreamily. She knew the other kids would tease her if she talked about fairies.

Her nana had said, "Avry, you get to decide what you believe in. Don't let anyone bully you into changing who you are."

Avry smiled so big at the thought of a fairy teacher that her dimples appeared. "A fairy teacher could give me wings, and I could fly to school. I wish I could do that instead of being on that noisy bus," she said to Marshmallow.

Avry sighed and pushed away the thoughts of school. Her nana would tell her to be in the moment. Avry was sensitive in so many ways.

She pushed her fingers into the soft fuzz of her oversized socks, and then put them on her feet. She felt the soft nightgown curled around her legs. She did not like tags, or tight things. She did not like anything scratchy.

Avry knew what she liked, but had a hard time saying it. Marshmallow meowed softly. He didn't yell or tell her to hurry. He didn't expect her to know where her glasses were. He didn't care when her backpack was lost under the lumpy orange chair on the sun porch. Marshmallow was content to let Avry be herself.

Marshmallow loved every bit of her, fly-away hair and all. When she was thinking about school, her insides got shaky. Marshmallow licked her hand and said, "Avry, we need some magic." He put a bubble of magic around them and filled it with soft swirling air. Avry relaxed.

When she was with Marshmallow, she loved to hear him purr as it rumbled from his chest. She wondered why she didn't purr. Then she realized the girls at school would think that was stupid. Avry tried not to care, but inside her feelings were hurt. "Marshmallow, why can't the other kids accept me the way I am?"

Marshmallow nuzzled in closer. Avry sighed. Avry knew that she and Marshmallow were happy together and that was enough for today.

Dr. Kimberly Brayman

Time Has Its Own Rules

Avry never could keep track of the days. Time, like magic, seemed to have its own set of rules. It could go fast, or dreadfully slow. Sometimes it would change its mind, and a day that seemed to stretch forever would suddenly be over.

"Marshmallow, why is time never the same? Everyone says to pay attention to the time, but it changes."

Marshmallow turned his head up, and then down. He was clearly thinking.

She loved the way he would turn his head just so, and how his crooked left ear would twitch.

Avry knew he was giving her a lesson on magic.

"Avry," he said, "cats and other magical beings do not feel it is important to worry about time. And you are magical."

Marshmallow licked his paw. That was all that needed to be said.

Avry's Magical Cat: A Marshmallow the Magic Cat Adventure

She wished the other kids at school would see that she was a magical being too. She knew that Stefan knew this about her.

Avry remembered that today, Stefan was going to Big White Mountain to ski. "Marshmallow, can magic ski? Or would it rather just dance in the gusty wind and watch the skiers?" Sometimes Avry thought magic was like a person, and sometimes she thought magic was an invisible energy.

Dr. Kimberly Brayman

She remembered what Stefan's dog, Shadow, had said. "Think of magic like the wind. You can't see it, but you can see what it does. Wind moves the water on the lake. magic makes unexpected wonderful things happen too."

Avry would miss seeing her friend, but she was happy Stefan was on the mountain. She hoped he saw magic skiing down the mountainside or dancing in the wind. Now that would be worth talking about!

"I wish I didn't have to struggle to keep track of time," Avry said. "The world is full of so many interesting things to focus on."

Marshmallow nodded in agreement. Avry knew that Stefan's dog Shadow would agree too.

"Stefan might have to keep track of time today," Avry said. She just hoped in her heart that magic would visit him on the mountainside.

Marshmallow reminded her, "Magic is everywhere, if you open your heart to look past the ordinary, and listen away from the noise."

Dr. Kimberly Brayman

Today Is the Day

Avry realized time had stretched out, and then shrunk, and then her mama came in and hugged her. A rosy glow filled her, and Avry wondered if it was sunshine or a bit of magic that filled her insides.

She didn't want to be hugged for too long, or have a hug that was too tight, but her mama's hugs were perfect.

She wondered if people knew how magical hugs were. She would ask Marshmallow.

"Nana is coming today," Avry's mama said, and the warm glow inside Avry grew and grew.

"Today!" Avry squealed.

Marshmallow turned one eye up and one down. "Avry, really, why do you need to be so loud?" Avry knew Marshmallow did not like loud noises.

"Marshmallow," Avry said, "our favorite magical person is coming today."

Then, as if by magic, she heard Nana's voice from downstairs. "Avry, Avry. Where are you, sleepy head? Nana is here to see you."

Nana Is Magical

Avry's Nana was a little odd. That's what her mama said. Avry knew odd meant magical. Nana had round pebbles in her pockets and paint in her suitcase. Nana looked at the owl and tree elves like Avry did, but most of the time she looked right inside of Avry. Nana had a lovely way of doing that.

"Nana is full of magic," Marshmallow said. "She's spent years sitting in woods, or by lakes with fairy folk." Avry remembered the many walks she and Nana took last summer.

"Avry, we need to talk to trees and flowers," Nana had said. "Then we need to listen. Only if we listen will we hear their whispered secrets." Avry wanted to hear the secrets too. She loved her walks with Nana.

Nana knew all the secret places to hide in the farmhouse. She and Avry sat in the attic on the dusty floor and drew unicorns and dragons. "It doesn't matter how dusty we get, Avry. It's the time we spend together that's important."

"Let me see your drawing, please," Nana said. She looked carefully at Avry's drawing.

"Nana," Avry said, "Do you know one of the things that makes me believe you are magical? You look at my drawings and you know how I feel inside." Nana smiled, and nodded.

"Let me tell you the story of Marshmallow," Nana said. Avry sat up in a flash and paid attention. "Marshmallow really is a magical cat from the land of the fairies and elves! He was coming to find you, when he was scooped up and taken to the animal shelter."

"Marshmallow knew where he was going," Avry said.

Nana agreed, "It is a good thing magic told your mama where to find him. Your mama hears magic, too," Nana said.

Avry nodded. "Sometimes she's so busy with work and errands that I think she forgets about magic."

Intuition

Avry said, "Mom, Marshmallow and I belong to each other. We belonged with each other, even before he came." Avry sat quietly for a moment, thinking. Then she added, "Sometimes we just know things."

"That is called intuition," her mama said thoughtfully, remembering the many moments she just knew things. "We all have it, if we listen inside, in our belly, even in our bones." Nana listened to them as she sipped her coffee.

"Avry," Nana said, "you were in my heart long before you were born." Avry smiled. Nana smiled. Her mama smiled. They all knew this was true.

Later, when her mama went to run errands, Nana stayed with Avry. "We need time here," she said. Her mama looked at the love between the two of them, and nodded.

Marshmallow said, "Avry, magic feels free to dance in the house with us. Let's bake cookies and have ice cream. Vanilla is my favorite!"

"It is the only one we give you," said Avry.

"That is why it is my favorite," said Marshmallow, and they all laughed.

Being Silly

Avry peered outside. "Too cold," she thought, not wanting to squish herself into snow pants and a jacket. "And I can never find my hat and mittens. They never stay in the wicker bin." Avry believed the fairies moved them. Her mama would smile and shake her head.

Marshmallow and Nana agreed that fairies moved things. Nana said, "They might not really be lost. Perhaps the fairies use your mittens as sleeping bags! Even if it was you who misplaced them, maybe an elf or little mouse might bring them back."

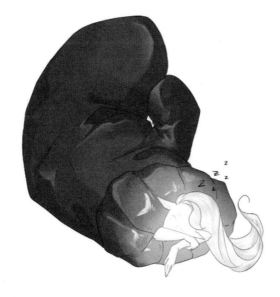

Before she knew it, Nana had worked her magic and Avry was outside rolling down the hillside and giggling. "Nana, I love the silly feeling in me when we roll and roll. It's cold, but it's fun too." Noses red and cheeks rosy, they ran inside to sit by the fire. Avry felt how precious love in a family was. She felt grateful, and the warm glow in her heart grew even bigger.

I Am Avry

"I am small when I'm beside Nana," Avry said. "Beside Marshmallow, I am big." She frowned and appeared puzzled.

Marshmallow said, "You are big and small. It is all about perspective. You can look at things in different ways, Avry."

Avry thought for a moment. Of course! When we are full of goodness, full of curiosity, and full of magic, we can be any size or shape. This was the magic her Nana wanted her to learn.

"Avry," Nana said, "every child is amazing and magical. You are amazing and magical."

Avry beamed. "You help me believe in myself," she said. "And you help me believe in magic." She felt loved.

Marshmallow blinked his green eyes. He knew, and she knew, this was a magical day. She could hardly wait for their next adventure.

Discussion Questions & Activities

1. Do you believe in magic? _____

    What does that mean to you? _____

    _____

    _____

2. Avry had a discussion on intuition with her mother. Do you ever just know something? _____

    Have you experienced intuition? _____

    What was it? _____

    _____

    _____

    _____

3. Get a piece of paper and draw a picture that shows how you are feeling right now. Drop your own self-judgment. Don't think that you have to fill up every second with words. Do this with friends and/or family. When everyone is done drawing, look closely and share with each other.

4. Do you have a pet that you love? _____
    What do they mean to you? _____

    _____

    _____

5. Nana and Avry spend a lot of time in nature. What does
    it feel like to sit in a sunny field, or walk down a road
    when the wind is blowing?" _____

    _____

    _____

    _____

6. Next time you go out for a walk, pay attention to what it
    feels like. It's good to spend time in nature. It can be in
    your backyard, a forest, or even on a balcony looking out
    at the beauty of nature.

7. Avry struggles with other girls at school. Do you get
    teased about anything? _____

    _____

    _____

    _____

8.   Do you feel like accepted for who you are? _____

What does it mean to you to be an individual? _____

_____

_____

_____

9.   Avry says she is both small and big. What do you think?

_____

_____

_____

_____

There is more than one way to look at everything. We can choose our perspective if we know this.

10.   Being an introvert means Avry has a hard time in groups, but it also means she is very sensitive, a deep thinker, and intuitive about others. Are you an introvert? _____

Why do you do think that? _____

_____

_____

_____

_____

11. Name something good that comes from doing things that are hard for you to do. _____

_____

_____

_____

12. Avry tells us about her friend, Stefan, in this story. What do you think about boys and girls being friends? _____

_____

_____

_____

_____

13. Do you have any friends that are not the same gender as you? _____

14. Does it matters what gender your friends are? _____
Why? _____

_____

_____

_____

_____

About the Author

Dr. Kimberly Brayman is a licensed psychologist in both Canada and the United States. After decades of working in health care she's inspired to build confidence, normalize struggle, inspire hope, and delight adults and children alike through her storytelling.

She believes stories build empathy and empower the listener to find their own self-reliance and strength. The power of supportive relationships is a strong theme. When a child knows deep in their heart that they are loved and accepted, just the way they are, they have a chance to blossom.

In this series, Avry is a highly sensitive, anxious girl who develops capability and courage, and gains insight with every adventure.

Her magic cat Marshmallow is her best friend and near-constant companion. They are joined by friends, family members and elves, fairies, animals and magic.

Dr. Kimberly Brayman is a registered psychologist (registration #2464) in British Columbia, Canada and a licenced psychologist (registration #3132) in Colorado, USA.

About the Illustrator

Irina Denissova loves creating illustrations for children's books. Her creative talents bring a magical atmosphere to stories, making them enjoyable for both parents and children. She believes the best part about being an illustrator is that she helps create a new world for readers.

She lives in Temirtau, Kazakhstan and, in her spare time, loves to read and create whatever drawings pop into her mind.

The author describes her as a humble, unbelievably talented young woman who has a near-magical ability to take her descriptions and characters and create what she sees in her mind.

Books by Dr. Kimberly Brayman

Young Readers Chapter Books
Marshmallow the Magic Cat Adventures

Avry and Atreus Save Christmas: A Marshmallow the Magic Cat Adventure.
A delightful Christmas tale to be read every holiday season. It's full of elves, ravens and the capability inside all children to redeem themselves and be good. Available in winter 2020.

A Troll in the Woods: A Marshmallow the Magic Cat Adventure
A true quest that shows courage and fear can go hand in hand, and the power of friendship to inspire action. Available on Amazon now.

Marshmallow Paints the Town: A Marshmallow the Magic Cat Adventure
A fun story that focuses on collaboration, self-responsibility, making mistakes and recovering. Coming Soon!

A Trip to the Hot Springs: A Marshmallow the Magic Cat Adventure
A lovely story with a focus on friendship, magic, and skills to assist with anxiety. Coming Soon!

Avry's Magical Cat: A Marshmallow the Magic Cat Adventure

Illustrated Children's Books

Nana Loves You More

Artsy Alphabet

Count With Me

Atreus and the Fisherman

Blueberries

Do I Have To?

I Am Different and I Am the Same

Visit the author's website at KimberlyBraymanAuthor.com for updates on when books are available at Amazon.

Avry's friend, Stefan, wants to find Avry the perfect birthday present. He ignores warnings from Marshmallow and the forest creatures and ventures into the forest alone. Stefan falls asleep and is taken by the Forest Troll. Stefan meets a family of skunks who try to help him. Will they be able to free Stefan? Will the Forest Troll stop them? Will Avry, Marshmallow and Shadow find Stefan in time? Available now on Amazon.

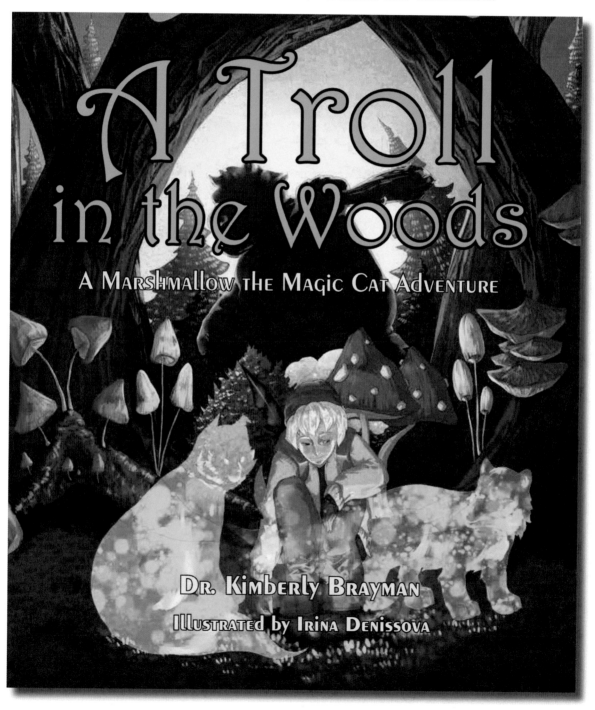

A Troll in the Woods

A Marshmallow the Magic Cat Adventure

Dr. Kimberly Brayman

Illustrated by Irina Denissova

Made in the USA
Monee, IL
24 October 2021